Jack the Cat
that Went to War

FORT SUMTER'S CAT

Written by Russell Horres, Jr.
Illustrated by Kate Sherrill

To Digger,

I hope you will enjoy Jack's story.

Russell Horres, Jr.

12/20/2011

*The author thanks friends and family for their enthusiastic support
and all the children who have been delighted in hearing about Fort Sumter's cat.*
—R.H.

*Thank you to God, who makes all things possible. Words cannot express my appreciation to my
amazing family, who gave me their support, encouragement, and patience throughout this project.
Special thanks to Kelly, whose cats Annie and Max were the primary models for Jack.
Thank you also to the many friends who helped in numerous ways—especially Ellen.
A very special thank you to Thea, whose superb modeling made June come to life,
and Mary Hatcher, who graciously shared her knowledge of period clothing.*
—K.S.

Jack the Cat That Went to War: Fort Sumter's Cat
Text copyright © 2011 by Russell Horres
Illustrations copyright © 2011 Kate Sherrill
Printed on acid-free paper in the USA. All rights reserved.
No part of this publication may be reproduced without the written consent of the author.
Published by High Battery Press
Charleston, SC

ISBN 978-0-615-43604-3

Cover design and book layout by Kate Sherrill.
All illustrations were rendered in oil on canvas.
Text is set in Goudy Old Style.

This book is dedicated to the staff at
Fort Sumter National Monument
and to all the children who come to visit.

Hello. My name is Jack. Jack the Cat, that is. I am a most unusual cat—not your typical lap-loving, purring type, but a real Johnny Reb of a cat. A true-blue, dyed in the wool Confederate Cat, that is. You see, I am the cat that went to war. Let me tell you all about that.

I was born a long, long time ago, over a hundred and fifty years they say, in a city by the sea called Charleston. My momma, Miss Kitty, told me that my grandparents came all the way from England on a real sailing ship. They had to work to pay their way to America by catching the mice hiding in the nooks and crannies of the ship. My dad, Mr. Tom, came from far away Ireland when the potato crops failed. Momma was a city cat and knew every street in Charleston, but Daddy was a country cat. He grew up on a rice plantation and only came to town in the summer to enjoy the parties.

"I am a most unusual cat."

What parties those were—the girls so beautiful in their wide silk dresses and the boys so handsome with waistcoats and vests. The music played and played, and the couples danced the night away. We cats never missed a party. You see, even way back then, they had ice cream, and lucky was the cat that got to lick the bowl! Well, that's how I grew up, never a care in the world and party after party.

We lived in a big house right by the water with lots of beautiful oak trees with long gray streamers of Spanish Moss hanging down. When the breeze blew off the harbor, the moss would sway back and forth as though the trees were dancing.

"What parties those were."

In back of the big house was a carriage house where they kept the horses and carriage, a barn for the cow that gave us milk, and lots of chickens to lay eggs. In the far back corner there was a bathroom—well, sort of, actually just a fancy hole in the ground—no indoor plumbing back then. We also had a house in the back where the slaves lived. The house was so tiny you could hardly believe that five people lived in each room. The slaves did all the work around the house. They boiled water in big black kettles to wash the clothes and hung them in the sun to dry. They fed and milked the cow, took care of the horses, cleaned the stables and swept the yard every day. Some of the slaves worked in the house where the Missus gave orders as to what needed cleaning each day. The Colonel was a wealthy man. He worked in a bank down on Broad Street a few blocks from our house.

Just behind the big house was the kitchen house. Back then, cooking fires were considered too dangerous to have in the big house, so all the cooking was done in the kitchen house. Visiting the kitchen house was a daily chore of mine. Mauma June ran that kitchen with an iron hand.

"There was a barn for the cow that gave us milk, and lots of chickens to lay eggs."

Mauma June was very wise and had beautiful dark brown skin and always wore a scarf around her hair. When I came by, she would order one of the other slaves who helped her in the kitchen to give me a bowl of milk. After a nice bowl of sweet, fresh milk, I would stretch out at Mauma June's feet while she worked on her sweetgrass baskets. She told me she was taught to weave baskets in far away Africa before she was captured by some bad men who sold her to the captain of a slave ship bound for America. Mauma June said she thought she was going to die on that ship, locked up with hundreds of others in the dark hold for over a month. When she got to Charleston, she was taken to an auction house and sold again to my master, Colonel Rhett. She was a young girl then, and the Colonel put her to work tending the fires in the kitchen. Every morning she had to get up before the sun came up and gather wood to start the fires so the stove would be ready to cook breakfast. She wasn't allowed to go to school, so she learned everything she could about cooking. Sometimes they would send her down to the market to buy food. To make sure she wouldn't run away, she had to wear a copper badge around her neck that indicated she was a slave. She was told that horrible things happened to slaves who tried to run away. As Mauma June's fingers wove that straw back and forth, she would tell me how much she missed her family in Africa and how lucky I was to have a family that loved me. Every once and awhile, she would whisper very softly in my ear so that no one could hear, "Someday Jack, I'm going to be free just like you."

"Mauma June's

One April morning back in 1861, I think it was the 12th, I was startled out of a sound sleep by a loud boom just before the sun came up. It was not raining, so I knew it could not be thunder. Soon boom followed boom until it began to sound like someone beating on a big drum. I thought I'd best go investigate the source of all this commotion, so I scampered down the steps and across the wide piazza (that's just a fancy name for a porch) to the garden. Out on the street it seemed that everyone was awake and hurrying down to the waterfront. I just had to find out what was going on. Curiosity, they say, causes us cats big problems.

"I scampered down to the garden."

What a racket the people were making! The horse-drawn carriages were going clippity-clop, clippity-clop along the cobblestone streets. Everyone was headed to the Battery, a wonderful park at the point of land where Charlestonians say the Ashley and Cooper Rivers come together to form the Atlantic Ocean. I sashayed between the crowds of people holding my tail high so no careless person would step on it. When I got to the Battery, there were so many people I could not even see what they were looking at. All the while the frightening booms rolled across the harbor. There was only one thing for a cat to do—climb up a big oak tree. Up I went, and every time I thought I had a view, that Spanish Moss was in the way.

Up, up, ever higher I went. Finally I found a branch without any moss that gave me

"It looked like fireworks."

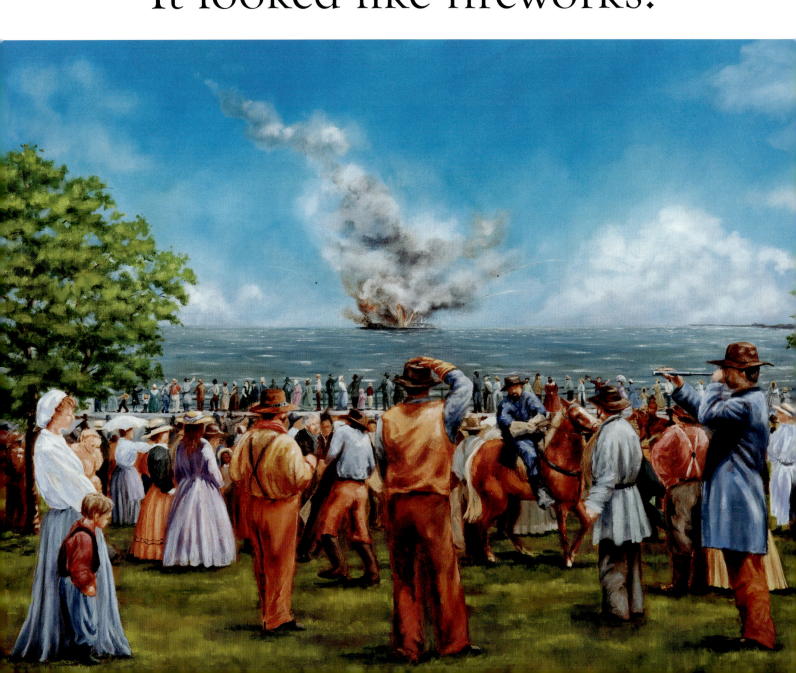

a wonderful view over the Battery sea wall. There, far out in the harbor, I saw where all the booms were coming from. It looked like a fireworks show except, instead of exploding high in the sky as they do on the 4th of July, the fireworks were exploding on a tiny island called Fort Sumter.

If you can believe it, that booming went on right around the clock. All day Friday it was boom after boom. When I checked things out on Saturday morning, huge clouds of smoke were billowing from that fort. It must have been terrible in there. Just after lunch, things got really quiet. I ran down to the Battery and up to my perch in the big oak tree. Small boats were crossing the harbor, and far out at Fort Sumter a white flag was flying. I thought, "Thank goodness! How's a cat to sleep with all that booming going on?"

"Up, up, ever higher I went."

The next day was Sunday and the church bells were ringing as usual. About noon the booming started again. This time it was really regular-like. I went back to my tree to see what was happening. The booms were coming from the fort as the American flag was being lowered. Someone shouted, "They are saluting the flag!" Fifty times the cannons boomed. A little while later, the flag I had seen with the soldiers here in Charleston was raised. "War! We are at war!" a boy shouted. "War," I wondered, "what does that mean?"

Well, it didn't take long to find out. That afternoon I overheard the Colonel say that the South no longer wanted to belong to the United States and had formed a new nation called the Confederate States of America. President Lincoln declared war because they had fired on United States soldiers in Fort Sumter. This meant Northern states would be fighting Southern states, and a lot of people were going to get hurt. Before long, all over town men in gray uniforms were joining the Confederate Army and marching to and fro. Mothers and children were crying as fathers left to fight in a place called Virginia.

As for me, I was having a great time because people were too busy with the war to worry about what a cat was up to. My favorite treat was to watch the ladies rolling bandages they tore from sheets and old petticoats. Every so often, someone would drop one, and I would pounce on it as it unrolled along the floor. There would be shouts of "Jack, leave that bandage alone!" but nothing was going to stop me from playing with my new toy as I bolted out the door with the bandage streaming behind me.

One day the Colonel said, "Jack, the Army needs you. Mice are causing big problems out at Fort Sumter. **"Jack, you have to do your duty."** They are eating the soldiers' food." I looked out at that fort, surrounded by all that water, and thought, "Jack, do you really want to do this?" I am afraid of water and, if I didn't have to drink, I would never go near it. "Don't worry, Jack," said the Colonel. "You will like it at the fort. There is plenty of food to eat and no dogs to chase you."

I was so afraid I ran to the kitchen and hid under Mauma June's calico skirt. Mauma June said, "Now Jack, the Colonel says the Army needs you, and you'll be fine out there. I'll give the Colonel this big sweetgrass basket for your bed."

The Colonel found me and said, "Come on now, Jack. You have to do your duty." Ever so reluctantly, I followed him to the beach where a rowboat with three strong slaves was waiting. He handed me down, and, thinking I might be able to jump out to the shore, I quickly climbed into the bow. The Colonel handed Mauma June's basket to one of the slaves and, while pushing off, got into the boat.

We were headed to Fort Sumter, over three miles away. The gentle rocking of the boat and the songs of the oarsmen put me sound asleep—a sort of catnap, you might say. "Bump!" went the boat as it hit the stone wharf and startled me awake. Refreshed from my nap, I bounded up the wharf and followed the Colonel through the sally port into Fort Sumter's headquarters. The Colonel called First Sergeant Langtry over and said, "Here is our new recruit. He is officially in the Army now. His name is Jack, and be sure to take good care of him."

He handed him the sweetgrass basket that Mauma June had made for my bed and returned to the boat. The fort was so big and dark that I was terrified and wanted to run back to the boat. But First Sergeant said, "Now come on, Jack, we've got a war to fight and everyone has to do their duty. Let me show you around the fort."

First he showed me the officers' quarters that lined the back wall and then the barracks on each side of the fort where the men lived. He told me that 200 men lived in each of the barracks and that in a moment's notice they could be at the guns lining the fort's walls. Then he took me into the back corner where he unlocked a heavy metal door. The door creaked as he pulled it open. It was very dark inside because there were no windows in the thick brick walls. First Sergeant said, "Jack, this is the powder magazine." Now that was a funny word to call a big cave. I thought a magazine was a kind of book. "Jack," he continued, "You must be very careful in here. There is enough gun powder stored in this magazine to blow us all to kingdom come." Locking the big door, he led me through a long passageway where we passed gun room after gun room called "casemates," each with a large cannon pointing out of a hole in the wall called an "embrasure."

"Here is our new recruit."

In the center of the fort, where the walls came to a point, was a circular stair tower. The First Sergeant bounded up the granite steps two at a time, and I could hardly keep up with my short legs. He stopped at the second level and told me that the bakery was on this floor, and that I would have to check it each day very carefully for mice because they were getting into the corn meal and flour. Back up the winding stairs he went until we reached the top.

Coming out of the stair tower into the bright sunlight, I had to pause a minute to adjust my eyes. Cats have very sensitive eyes, you know, so that we can catch mice in the dark. Before me were huge cannons on wooden carriages pointing out to sea. They looked very scary to me. Seagulls and pelicans soared above the walls, and the sea crashed against the rocks down below. I couldn't see the water because a sturdy brick wall about four feet tall surrounded the top of the fort. First Sergeant said, "Now, Jack, I want you to be very careful when you come up here. Just look behind you." Slowly, I turned around and my heart almost stopped as I realized I was on the edge of a flat roof without a railing or anything to prevent me from falling 40 feet to the ground below. First Sergeant said, "Jack, this is called the terreplein, and we depend on the rainwater that falls here for our drinking water. See those large clay pipes that run down the walls? They channel the water into underground cisterns. That is all well and good, Jack, but do you see those seagulls flying around? They make a mess up here, and you can hardly drink the water because of it. Your duty, Jack, is to scare them away."

"Do you see all those gulls?"

First Sergeant Langtry said, "Well, Jack, we've seen the fort, but before we go down, there is something else I want you to see." He motioned me to jump up on top of one of the big cannons that pointed over the brick wall. I hopped on the lower wooden carriage and then climbed to the sloping top carriage, up to where the trunnions held the big gun in place. From there it was a short hop to the barrel.

I was now above the brick wall they called the parapet that had blocked my view. It was as if the whole world opened up before me! Looking west, I could see Charleston and almost make out my home on the Battery. Looking east out into the ocean, I could see many ships on the horizon. First Sergeant said, "Jack, those are the enemy ships of the United States Navy. They are blockading our port to stop ships from bringing us supplies, gunpowder and weapons. Sometimes in the dead of night, though, our ships will slip in. We call them blockade runners. Now, Jack, if there's any trouble, it will come from those Navy ships. Before you start shooing away those gulls, you'd better be sure to check on those ships."

Quickly I settled into my routine patrols. Three times each day I would climb the stair tower to the terreplein, hop up on a cannon, check on the ships, and begin running around the five sides of the fort as fast as I could go. My, how those gulls would squawk when they saw me coming! Then, when I had finished the entire pentagon, it was back down the winding stairs and back to headquarters for a much-deserved nap. I had to get most of my sleeping in the daytime, for at night I was constantly prowling the mess halls and dark gun casemates for mice. Within a couple of weeks, I had things completely under control. Not a mouse remained in all of Fort Sumter. Then the problem was, without mice, what was I to eat?

"Looking into the ocean, I could

see many ships on the horizon."

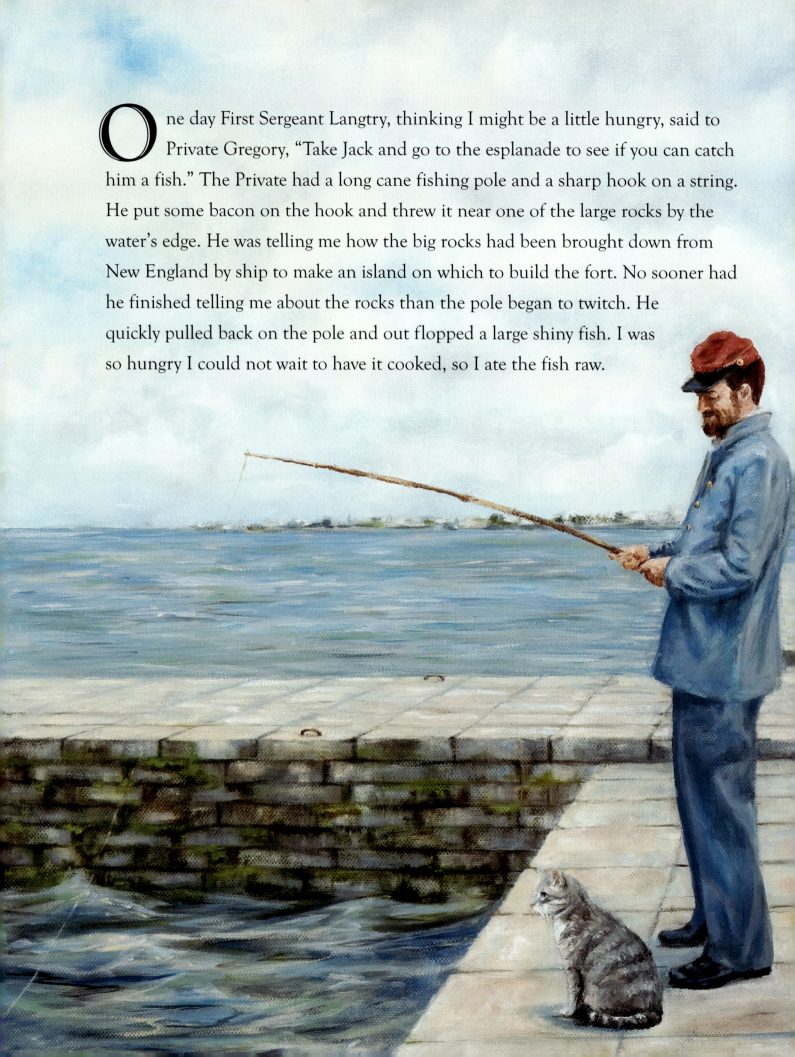

One day First Sergeant Langtry, thinking I might be a little hungry, said to Private Gregory, "Take Jack and go to the esplanade to see if you can catch him a fish." The Private had a long cane fishing pole and a sharp hook on a string. He put some bacon on the hook and threw it near one of the large rocks by the water's edge. He was telling me how the big rocks had been brought down from New England by ship to make an island on which to build the fort. No sooner had he finished telling me about the rocks than the pole began to twitch. He quickly pulled back on the pole and out flopped a large shiny fish. I was so hungry I could not wait to have it cooked, so I ate the fish raw.

"Take Jack to the esplanade to see if you can catch him a fish."

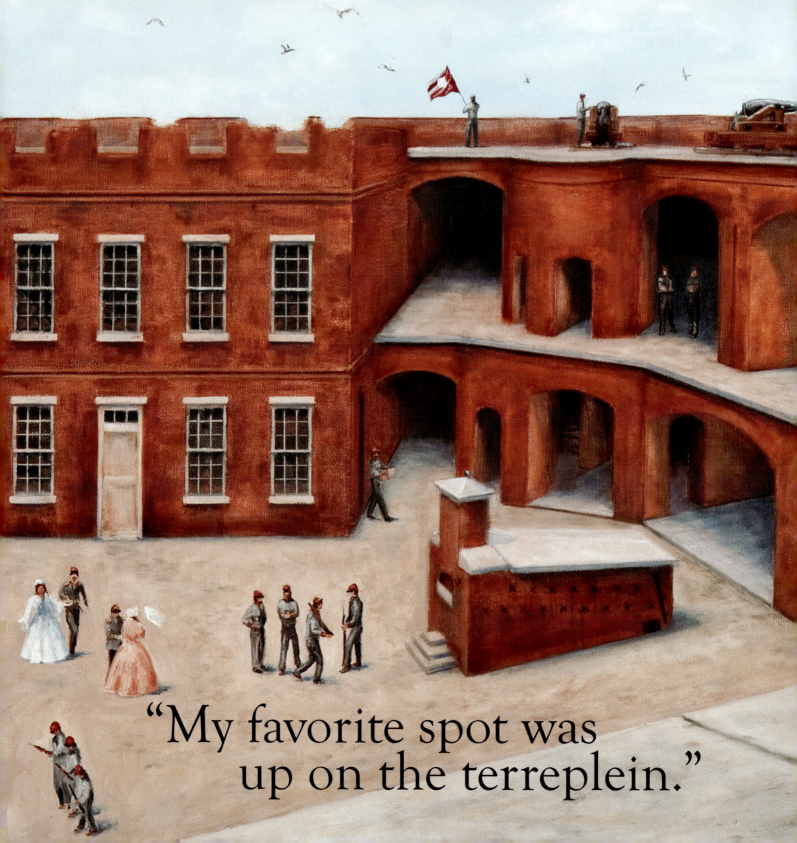

Those were the best of days out at Fort Sumter. There was plenty to eat, and parties were held several times a month when the men from Fort Moultrie were invited over. My favorite day was Friday. A boat load of ladies would arrive from the city in their beautiful silk dresses, and soon the brass band would strike up a march.

"My favorite spot was up on the terreplein."

The men in their best uniforms would parade back and forth on the field in the middle of the fort. I guess that's why they call it the "parade." My favorite spot to watch the parade was up on the terreplein. The visitors were so impressed. They said that the garrison was the best they had ever seen.

Except on lonely nights when I missed my family and Mauma June's bowls of milk, I began to think that this war business was not too bad after all. Then one day everything changed. It was in early April, and the weather had begun to warm up. I noticed that the men had on their best uniforms and that the band had assembled. The beautiful flags were run up the tall pole, and the band struck up "Dixie," the favorite song of the garrison. Wondering what all the commotion was about, I scampered up the circular stair tower and up to the parapet. The men were already standing by the big guns, and the orderlies were bringing powder bags called cartridges from the powder magazines.

In a bound, I sprung up on the nearest of the cannons to see what all the fuss was about. The soldiers shouted, "Get down from there, Jack!" Like most cats, I seldom follow orders, so I stole a look out to sea. There, in the middle of the channel, were seven dark ships with black smoke billowing out of their smokestacks. They were flying the same United States flag that used to fly over Fort Sumter before the war. They had come to attack our fort. I heard the Colonel say, "Ready, aim, fire!" All of a sudden, the gun next to me leapt backwards and blew out fire and smoke. The noise really hurt my ears. Pretty soon, guns all over the harbor started booming, and the water all around those ships was rising up in huge columns as the shot from the cannons fell all around.

Then I saw a flash from one of the low ships with a round box on it, and the men yelled, "Get down, Jack, they are firing back!" I didn't have a clue as to what they were fussing about. Then in a blink of an eye, a loud crash hit the wall right beneath my perch. It was as though lightning had struck. Bricks were flying everywhere. The whole fort shook and knocked me off the cannon. I could hardly see from all the smoke. I was so scared all I could think about was the sweetgrass basket that Mauma June said would keep me safe. Down the winding stairs I ran. I started across the parade when I heard someone shout, "Jack, don't go out there. It's not safe!"

"Safe?" I thought, "What could be worse than being up there on that parapet?" Since, like all cats, I am somewhat of a hard head, I kept running. I heard a crash against the bricks and saw a large hissing ball drop into the parade. I froze in my tracks, not knowing what to do—scared stiff, as they say. Then there was a flash and a loud "KA-BOOM!" I was knocked for a loop. The next thing I heard was men shouting, "Jack's been hurt." Someone else said, "He's dead."

"Jack, don't go out there.

It's not safe!"

I lay there on the ground for a moment, catching my breath, and then sprang to my feet and ran back into the protection of the casemate. No more short cuts for me! I went all the way around the fort under the cover of the thick casemates to reach headquarters. Still dusty from my encounter with the shell, I nevertheless took to the safety of Mauma June's basket, high atop the Commander's desk. For two-and-a-half hours the fight went on. With every boom I would get a little lower in my bed. Then I heard the men shouting with joy, "The Navy's been beaten! We won the battle!"

When the Colonel came into the office, he said, "Has anyone seen Jack? I heard that he got hurt." Corporal Cooper smiled, pointed to my basket, and said, "He's okay, but you better check on Will Ahrens, the drummer boy. A piece of that shell hit him in the head, and he's bleeding badly."

The Colonel said, "Jack, you scaredy cat! Why are you hiding in there? Come on down and join the party."

No way, no how! I wasn't going to budge. It wasn't till long after dark, when they brought the slaves over and made them repair the fort, that I even dared to come out of my basket to take a look around.

Well, after that exciting day, things returned to normal. Spring passed, and the heat of summer set in. With no more shooting, I pretty much picked up my old routine. First I would check for mice in the kitchens and bakery. Then I went up the winding stairs to shoo away the seagulls. Life was boring, but it was sure better than being blown to smithereens. One hot August day, I had just checked out the bakery on the second floor of the northwest corner. Then, in a blink of an eye, an explosion occurred, and loaves of bread went flying everywhere. There were no ships around, so I didn't think it could have been cannon fire. The U.S. Army had been fooling around on the southern end of Morris Island, but they were way too far away for those guns to reach the fort. "Boy," I thought, "that was some mistake in the dough. Did they use gunpowder instead of flour?"

Then another explosion occurred against the inside wall, and drummer boy Johnny Graham, who had been standing in the sally port, was struck down by a piece of shell. Fort Sumter was not safe for drummer boys or cats, for that matter. No more thoughts about exploding bread—Fort Sumter was under attack. You can guess where I headed—back to my basket!

"Jack, you scaredy-cat!"

When I got back to headquarters after taking the long way around, I heard the Colonel discussing with the officers about where those shots could have come from. One of them said he saw the gun when it fired the second shot, and it was over two miles from Fort Sumter where the U.S. Army had been working. I have never seen such an expression on the Colonel's face. He stared at the floor for the longest time, and in a low and sad voice he said, "Men, we have to get the gun powder out of the magazines. They are attacking us with those new rifled guns against our weakest side—the gorge wall. If they keep up the shelling, the wall will collapse in a matter of days."

During the next couple of days, the sounds were awful as shell after shell slammed into the bricks. Slowly, bit by bit, the fort was being knocked down around us. Even though I was curled up in my basket, there was no sleeping, for every few minutes the orderly would come in and report that some soldier had been injured or killed. Every night soldiers and slaves would work all night carrying the heavy barrels of powder to boats that would take the powder back to Charleston. On their way back to the fort they would be carrying sandbags and cotton bales to plug the holes made by the artillery shells. The once-mighty cannons were heaved over the parapet walls to the rocks below where they could be moved to other forts in the harbor.

It was no longer safe for me to go on my patrols for mice and, with all the noise, I doubted whether the seagulls would ever come back. Besides, the terreplein was wrecked, so there would be no way to collect water anymore.

The Colonel said, "Jack, we are going to have to move headquarters. This area is just not safe anymore. We'll set you up a new place over by the small postern door. You'll like it there. You'll be able to look out at the harbor, and the walls are extra thick there next to the magazine. No need to worry about all this shelling over there."

"The walls are extra thick next to the magazine."

We were pretty comfortable over in the corner of the fort, as comfortable as you could be with nearly constant explosions and shells dropping in. The fort was now a big pile of rubble. The marching band was gone, as was the artillery regiment. Then I got a new master because Colonel Rhett left with his regiment to fight the Yankees back on the mainland. I wished they had taken me. Fort Sumter was now just an infantry post with only a couple of cannons to guard the harbor. The men just had rifles to defend what was left of the fort.

Other than an attempt by the U.S. Navy and Marines to storm the fort in small boats one night, things were pretty quiet except for the artillery. Now that it was impossible to catch mice, the men started feeding me from their supper, and I began to get fat and lazy. On Monday we had cornbread and bacon. On Tuesday we had bacon and cornbread. On Wednesday it was back to cornbread and bacon. On Thursday—you guessed it. Every once and awhile someone would bring me a fish that had been blown out of the water by a shell that fell short. To make myself useful, I took to standing guard at the postern gate with the sentry. He would say, "Halt! What is the sign for the day?"

Even when he let people enter, I would give them a good sniffing to make sure no Yankee spies tried to sneak in.

You will not believe what happened next! One crisp December morning, I was up early doing guard duty. The men, waiting to get their daily ration of cornbread and bacon, were lined up in the passage leading from the powder magazine. I heard a muffled roar and men crying out, and then headquarters filled with smoke. It took awhile for the commander to figure out that the magazine had exploded. There was no enemy fire that morning, so it must have been an accident. Many men were badly hurt, some died, and our headquarters was ruined.

"The fort was now a big pile of rubble."

I thought this would be the end of my stay at Fort Sumter, but those Confederates would never give up the fort. They just moved headquarters about five casemates away and fixed it up really nice. Without a cannon, there was plenty of room. They built a bunk bed for the commander, and he brought a high-backed rocking chair over from the city. A real window was added to the embrasure to keep out the wind, and a pot-bellied stove kept everything toasty in the winter. The fort's desk was placed against the wall and, as usual, Mauma June's sweetgrass basket was placed high on top just like I liked it. We had hardly gotten settled in our new quarters when we got another commander. Actually, Captain Mitchell wasn't really new. He had been at the fort for years. But just to show you how dangerous it was to live at Fort Sumter, poor Captain Mitchell was killed by an exploding shell just two-and-a-half months later while he was using his telescope to spot the enemy. That same day Captain Thomas Huguenin was sent over from Fort Moultrie to be our new commander. Most people could not pronounce his name, so we called him "Captain H." He was the youngest of the fort's commanders but a very kind man. He and I spent many days and nights together in the cozy new headquarters.

We didn't know it at the time, but the war was almost over. The Union Army was adding more black soldiers, and the South's armies were losing men they couldn't replace. The Confederates at Fort Sumter were more determined than ever to hold on to the fort, no matter what. Slaves were forced to work on strengthening the battered walls and digging tunnels through the great mounds of bricks that once were forty-foot-high walls. By Christmas, in many ways, Fort Sumter was stronger than ever. Artillery fire no longer had any serious effect on the fort because the men were living deep underground.

As the winter months rolled on, I spent a lot of time perched in the window that had been built into the old gun embrasure. From there I could see the church steeples in Charleston on a sunny day and watch for the supply boats that came every evening with food and water. I really put on a lot of weight that winter. It was no use going on mouse patrols anymore, and the men fought over who got to bring me food—mostly corn bread and bacon, but who could complain?

"I could see the church steeples in Charleston."

I was finally getting used to being at war. I knew everyone in the fort, and I sort-of felt that it belonged to me since I had been there longer than most of the men. Speaking of long, this terrible war had been going on for almost four years. Then, on the evening of February 17, 1865, a date I will never forget, the men gathered up all their belongings and began boarding boats for Charleston. I knew something was up and followed Captain H. as he checked on every detail and made sure no one was left behind. When we reached the flag pole, with my sharp eyes I could see that the flag was still flying. He turned to leave, and I let out a loud meow to get his attention. He said, "Jack, I know the flag is still up. We want to leave it flying to confuse the Yankees into thinking that we are still here."

By this time, only Captain H. and I were left in the fort. I thought of all the days and nights I had spent in the fort and of all the men who had fought to hold on to Sumter. It was a sad time, but I looked up at the starry sky and thought, "Jack, it's time to move on." Captain H. called out, "Come on, Jack. We have to leave." He was about to close the gate when I thought about my basket. I ran back to headquarters and pulled it off the desk, and with all my strength I dragged it to the gate where Captain H. picked it up and placed it in the bottom of the boat. Captain H. then picked me up and passed me down to waiting hands. I climbed into the bow for the long row back to Charleston. This time, there was no sleeping in the rocking boat, for huge explosions lit up the night sky, and fires were burning in the city. They said the Confederates were destroying everything the Yankees could use. When the boat reached the wharf, Captain H. told his men to go ahead and then picked me up, basket and all. He said he was going to take me home.

"Huge explosions lit up the night sky."

"He passed me through the car to all the soldiers I served with at Fort Sumter."

Charleston looked so different from what I had remembered. Four years of war had left its mark. When we got to our house, everything was dark. Captain H. placed the basket on the piazza, petted me on the head, and said, "Jack, I don't know where your folks have gone. You'll just have to wait here." He turned and headed toward the train station. I stood all alone there on that dark, cold piazza and watched him disappear. I wondered what I would do now. "This won't do!" I thought as I dashed for the train station. When I got there, there was a mob of soldiers and people trying to leave town. Everyone was talking about General Sherman's huge army that was marching toward Columbia, just 100 miles away. How would I even find my unit in the crowd? Suddenly, I caught a glimpse of an officer boarding the train, and I knew it must be Captain H. With every ounce of strength I had left, I leapt onto the train car. It was Captain H., and boy, was he surprised to see me! He stooped down and picked me up. He said, "Jack, you were supposed to wait at the big house." I just meowed back. He could tell that I wanted to go with him.

He then said, "Jack, you have been a brave cat and have done your duty. This war will be over soon, and peace will come back to Charleston. You belong here." He passed me through the car with all the soldiers I had fought with at Fort Sumter. Everyone gave me a gentle pet, and then they passed me back to Captain H. Just then, I heard my name called, "Jack! Is that you, Jack?" It was Mauma June! I would have recognized that voice anywhere. Captain H. handed me down to those wonderful strong hands that had petted me so many times. The train whistle blew, and the engine chugged and chugged as the train slowly began to move. I glanced back at the car, and all the men were saluting me and shouting, "Jack, we'll see you when the war is over!"

Mauma June held me tight as we watched the train disappear in the darkness. She said, "Jack, let's go back to the big house. Everyone left down there when the shelling started. It just wasn't safe. But with these Confederates gone, I'll bet the shelling will stop." All I could think about was the nice bowl of milk she always had for me.

Mauma June carried me all the way back to the Battery. I was glad for the help, since I was pretty tired from all the excitement. When we got to the house, she saw my basket on the piazza and said, "Jack, you can't stay out here. You'll freeze to death." She picked up my basket, carried it back to the kitchen house, and placed it next to the oven. She fussed about with some wood and matches and soon had a nice fire going. It didn't take long for the little house to get warm as toast. Mauma June said, "Jack, the cows have been gone for almost two years now, so I have no milk for you, but I do have some nice bacon and corn bread one of the soldiers gave me before they left."

What was a hungry cat to do? After a dinner of my favorite food, I jumped up into Mauma June's lap and slept better than I could ever remember. Sometime in the night Mauma June must have put me in my basket, but I certainly don't remember it. All I know is that I was startled out of my basket by a strange voice shouting, "Is there anybody in here?" Standing in the doorway was a tall black man in a United States Army uniform with a rifle that had the longest shiny bayonet that I had ever seen. I didn't know whether to hide or run.

Mauma June said, "Ain't nobody in here but a slave and this old gray cat. Please don't shoot us!"

He removed the scary bayonet and said, **"You are free now."** "Oh no, ma'am, I don't mean to do you and your cat any harm. We've been out there on Morris Island for the last two years fighting those Confederates so we could set you free."

Mauma June said, "What do you mean, set me free? You fool, it takes a lot of money to free a slave."

The soldier said, "Oh no, ma'am, haven't you heard that President Abraham Lincoln promised to free all the slaves when this war is done?" Mauma June did not know what to say. She asked the soldier if he wanted a cup of coffee. He said, "No ma'am, General Foster told me to tell every slave in Charleston that they are free. I've got to be going. There are lots of slaves to tell." Then he was gone.

Mauma June turned back and put more wood in the oven. She was mumbling something I could not hear. I purred a little and rubbed up against her leg. She turned around and picked me up. Then I saw tears streaming down her face. She said, "Jack, I'm so happy—I'm free again!"

Well, that's how the war ended for me. I wish I could tell you that life was good again soon, but there were lots of hard times for Charleston after the war. Many of the men in gray who marched off in 1861 never came back, so there were lots of boys and girls who never knew their fathers. Men who were once young now looked so old, and many of them had lost an arm or leg in battle. The city was practically destroyed, and work was hard to find. When the Missus came back to the big house, she told Mauma June that she had to pay rent to stay in the kitchen house. The Colonel lost everything in the war, and she had to make some money. Mauma June said she didn't have any money, so the Missus told her to leave and to take that old cat with her.

Mauma June moved up town to a small house where we shared a room with another family, and she made money by doing laundry for other people. I'm getting old now and spend most of my days sleeping in this old basket, but every day Mauma June brings me a bowl of fresh milk and picks me up afterwards for a nap in her soft lap. Every once and a while, Mauma June and I take a stroll down to the Battery and look out over the sea wall to Fort Sumter. I remember the good times and the bad times I had out there during that terrible war. I'm indeed a lucky cat to have gone to war and survived. You know, I guess it's true what they say about cats—we really do have nine lives.

The Real Story of Fort Sumter's Cat

Although no written evidence has been found, both oral tradition and period drawings support the existence of a garrison cat at Fort Sumter during the Civil War. The illustrations in which the cat appears definitively place the cat in the fort between December of 1863 and December of 1864. In both illustrations the cat is in the correct location for the fort headquarters at that time. According to oral tradition attributed to Confederate engineer John Johnson, the cat was there during the major bombardments of the fort and would take cover in a straw basket during the bombardments. Oral tradition also holds that Jack was a favorite of the garrison, who fought over who was going to feed him. We have used names of figures associated with the fort and included actual events for historical accuracy. Details of the cat's home and association with historical figures are fictionalized.

GLOSSARY *of terms used in Jack the Cat*

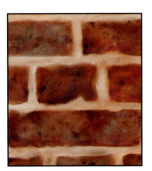

BAYONET & SCABBARD

GRAY BRICK

COLUMBIAD CANNON

EMBRASURE

ESPLANADE

Barracks: Buildings for housing troops in a fort. Fort Sumter's two barracks housed 400 soldiers.

Bayonet: A long, knife-like metal tip placed on the end of a rifle to turn it into a kind of spear. When not in use, the bayonet was stored in a protective sheath known as a scabbard.

Battery (Charleston): When a group of cannons are placed together, they are called a battery. Charleston's long sea wall is called "the Battery" because of the cannons once placed there.

Captain: In the army, captain is a military rank two levels below colonel. A captain usually commands a company of 100 soldiers.

Cannon: A large metal tube for firing heavy projectiles. Fort Sumter had a number of 8-inch and 10-inch Columbiad cannons that fired round solid balls or powder-filled shells. All of Fort Sumter's cannons were muzzle-loading, which means that the powder cartridge was loaded in the muzzle before the projectile.

Cartridge: A bag, usually made of silk, that held a measured amount of gun powder.

Casemate: Strong rooms in a fort where cannons were placed to fire through embrasures. When Fort Sumter was destroyed by artillery, the men and Jack lived in the remaining casemates.

Charleston Gray Brick: A type of brick made from clay found in the Charleston, South Carolina area. Most of the bricks in Fort Sumter are Charleston Gray bricks made by slaves.

Columbiad: A type of heavy smoothbore cannon invented in 1811 and widely used in sea coast defense.

Colonel: Colonel is an army rank that usually commands 1,000 soldiers. The next higher rank is general. Fort Sumter was commanded by a colonel.

Corporal: The next rank up from a private in the army.

Drummer Boys: Young boys trained to give drum signals to the troops during battles. Fort Sumter had two drummer boys injured by exploding shells during the Civil War.

Embrasure: An opening in a wall or parapet through which cannons were fired. Jack liked to sit in an embrasure.

Esplanade: An open, level area next to a body of water. Jack went fishing on the esplanade.

Fuse: A device used to explode powder-filled shells either by time or on contact.

Garrison: All the officers and men who defend a fort.

Gorge: The rear wall of a fort. In Fort Sumter, the officers' quarters were along the gorge.

Gun Carriage: A gun carriage is a sturdy frame of wood or metal that holds a cannon in position and allows it to be aimed and fired at a target. At Fort Sumter, the carriages were built in two parts. When the cannon fired, the top carriage would slide backwards along the bottom carriage. This is known as recoil.

Hot Shot Furnace: An oven-like structure designed to heat cannon balls "red hot" for firing at wooden ships. Fort Sumter had two hot shot furnaces.

Ironclad: Wooden ships covered, or clad, with iron plates to protect them from cannon fire.

Lieutenant: The lowest rank of an officer in the army.

Magazine: A protected place where gunpowder or ammunition is stored. Fort Sumter's powder magazines were in the back corners of the gorge wall on the first and second levels.

Mess Hall: A place where soldiers eat.

Officer: A person who has leadership authority in the military.

Officers' Quarters: Buildings for housing officers in a fort.

Parade: Open area in a fort where parades are held.

Parapet: A wall at the top edge of a fort to protect the men behind it.

Pentagon: A shape with five straight sides. Fort Sumter was built in the shape of a pentagon.

Piazza: In Charleston, it is a large porch on the side of a house.

Private: The lowest rank in the army.

Rifle: A cannon with spiral grooves in its bore that caused the projectile to spin. Rifled cannons fired elongated shells and shot, instead of balls, and were more accurate than smoothbore cannons.

Sally Port: The main gate of a fort.

Sergeant: The next military rank above a corporal in the army.

Shell: A hollow projectile containing an explosive material.

Shot: A solid projectile.

Spanish Moss: A plant common to oak trees in the South that grows in long hair-like gray strands.

Tier: A level of guns in a fort. Fort Sumter had three tiers of guns.

Terreplein: The level area at the top of the fort where cannons were placed.

Trunnions: Round projections from the sides of a cannon that hold it in the carriage and allow the cannon barrel to move up and down.

Traverse Rails: Curved flat-iron plates upon which a gun carriage's wheels moved in order to aim at a target.

Wharf: A structure that extends into a body of water to allow ships to load and unload cargo.

HOT SHOT FURNACE

MAGAZINE

PIAZZA

SALLY PORT

SHELL WITH BURNING FUSE